This book belongs to

.

_____

_____

For Charlie and Lucas — all the inspiration a
dad could wish for
I. R.

To my little stars R, E and J
I. N.

First published in Great Britain in 2005 by Gullane Children's Books
This paperback edition published in 2006 by
Gullane Children's Books
an imprint of Pinwheel Limited
Winchester House, 259-269 Old Marylebone Road,
London NW1 5XJ

1 3 5 7 9 10 8 6 4 2

Text © Ian Robson 2005
Illustrations © Ian Newsham 2005

The right of Ian Robson and Ian Newsham to be identified as the author and illustrator of this work
has been asserted by them in accordance with the Copyright, Designs and Patents Act, 1988.
A CIP record for this title is available from the British Library.

ISBN-13: 978-1-86233-614-8
ISBN-10: 1-86233-614-8

Printed and bound in China

The Star
who fell out
of the sky

Ian Robson · Ian Newsham

GULLANE
CHILDREN'S BOOKS

It was night and the jungle animals were sitting
around the camp fire, looking at the stars.
Suddenly Harold the Hippo saw something unusual.

"Look everybody," he said, "that
star looks like it is falling out of the sky!"
The animals looked up. There was a star falling out of
the sky, heading straight for their fire. The animals
watched as it grew bigger and bigger . . .

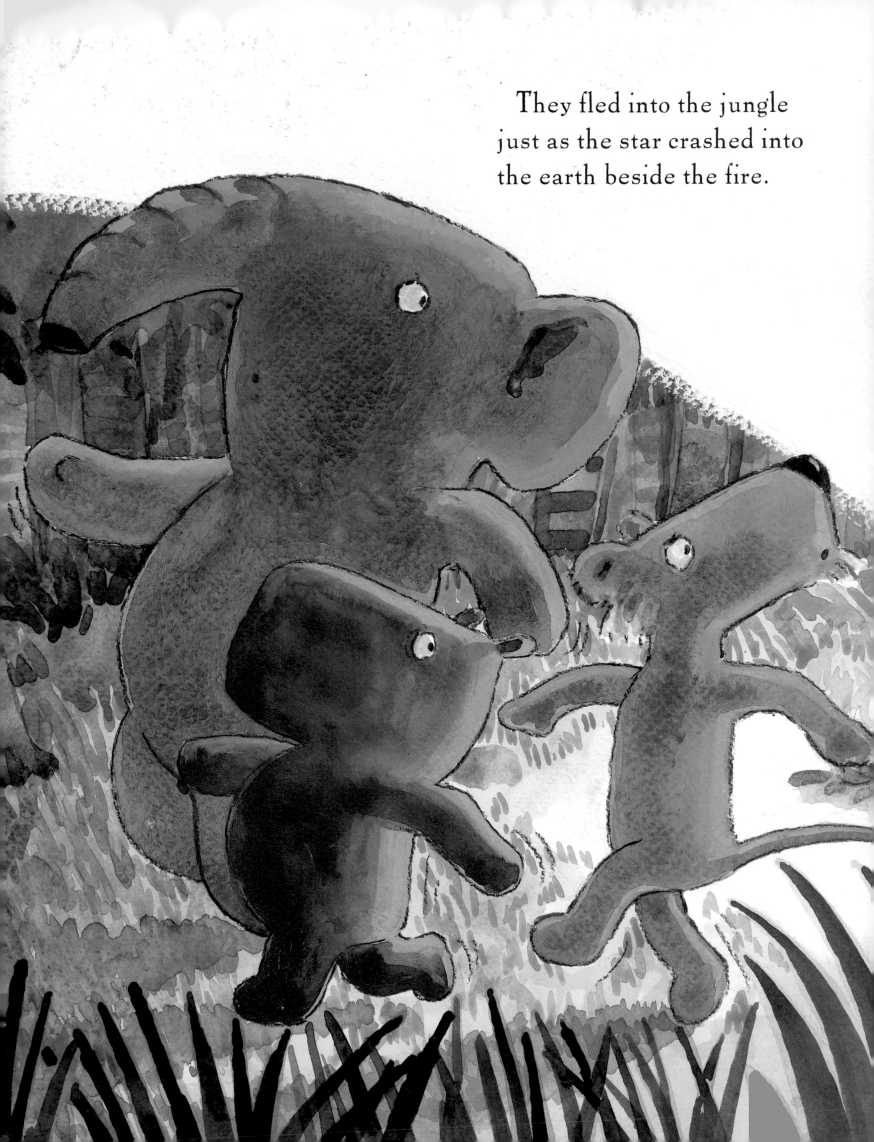

They fled into the jungle just as the star crashed into the earth beside the fire.

"Ouch!"
said the star.

One by one the animals appeared until they were
all gathered around the star.
"What happened to you?" roared Leonard the Lion.
"I fell out of the sky of course!" said the little star, "and
I really hurt myself when I landed." The star began to cry.
He was very sad. "How can I get back to my friends now?"
he moaned.

"I have an idea . . ." said Harold shyly.

"Don't be silly," scolded Leonard, "you never have good ideas.
I will have to have an idea." All the animals turned to Leonard.
"I am the strongest animal in the jungle," he boasted, "so I will
pick up the star and throw it as hard as I can back into the sky."

The little star looked worried by this idea but he agreed to do as Leonard said. The lion picked up the star . . .

and threw him as hard as he could up into the sky.

The star got smaller and
smaller as it flew higher
and higher into the sky.

Soon it was almost the same
size as all the other stars.

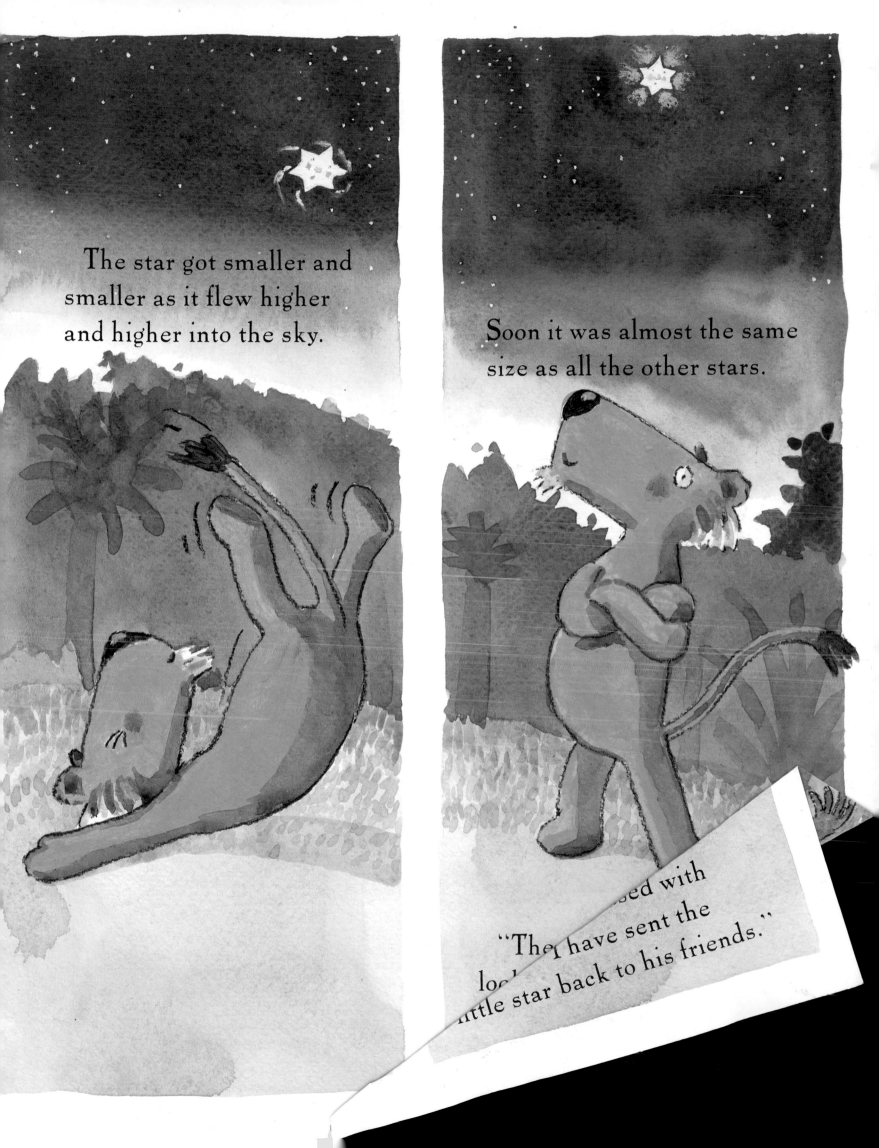

"The have sent the
loo...   ...sed with
little star back to his friends."

But, as the animals watched,
the star began to get bigger . . .
and bigger. It was falling back
towards the jungle.
    The animals ran for cover.

Once again the little star landed with a heavy thump.
"Ouch, that *really* hurt!" he said.
"I'm sorry," said Leonard. "I did my best. Now I
don't know *how* we can get you back up into the sky."

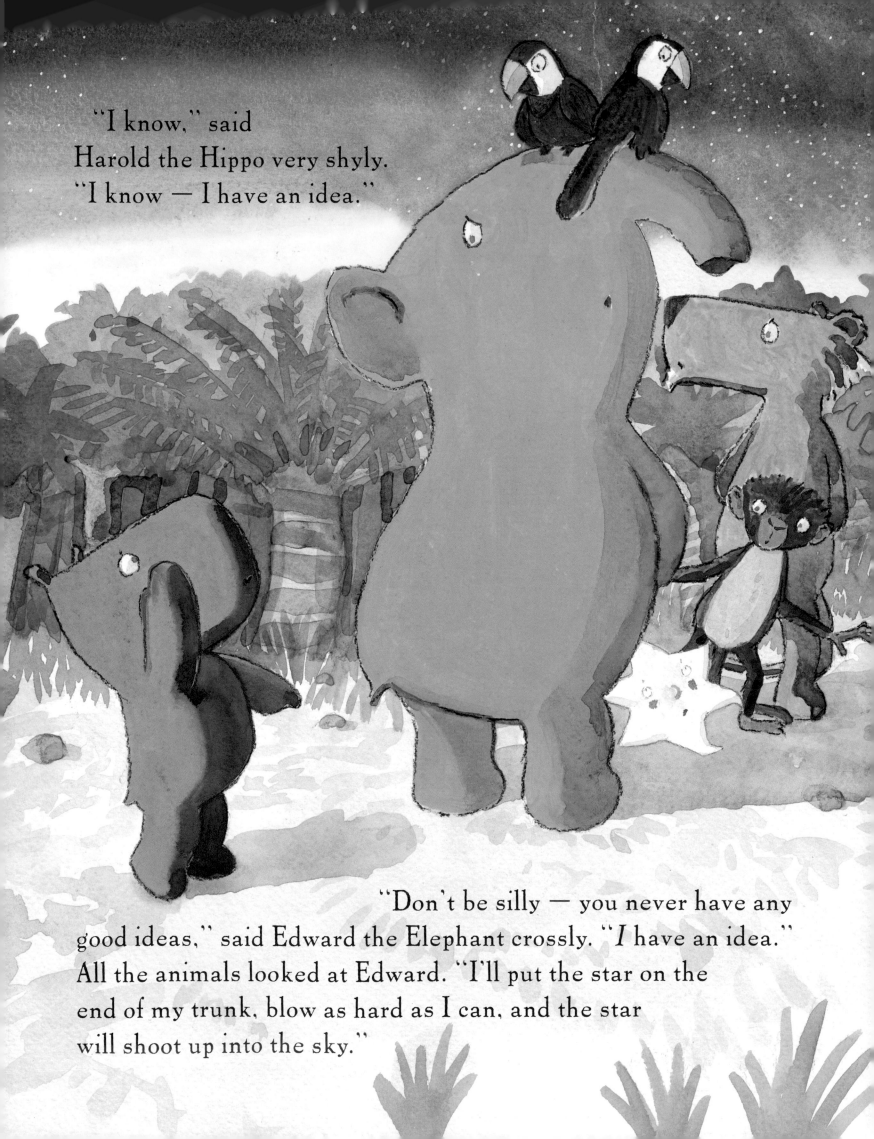

"I know," said
Harold the Hippo very shyly.
"I know — I have an idea."

"Don't be silly — you never have any
good ideas," said Edward the Elephant crossly. "*I* have an idea."
All the animals looked at Edward. "I'll put the star on the
end of my trunk, blow as hard as I can, and the star
will shoot up into the sky."

For the second time the star looked worried. But once more he agreed to the plan. Edward picked him up, put him on the end of his trunk . . .

and blew out a great big breath of air.

The star rose up into the sky,
getting smaller and smaller
until it was almost the same
size as the other stars.

The star stopped for a
moment and Edward looked
very pleased. "There you
are," he said. "I've done it!"

"Uh-oh!" said Milly Monkey as the star began to fall back towards the camp fire. "No you haven't."

The star landed hard beside the
animals. "Ouch and ouch again,"
said the star, "this is getting silly."

This time, before Harold could say a word, Percy and
Pandora the parrots squawked together. "We have an idea.
We can lift up the little star and fly him back up to his friends."

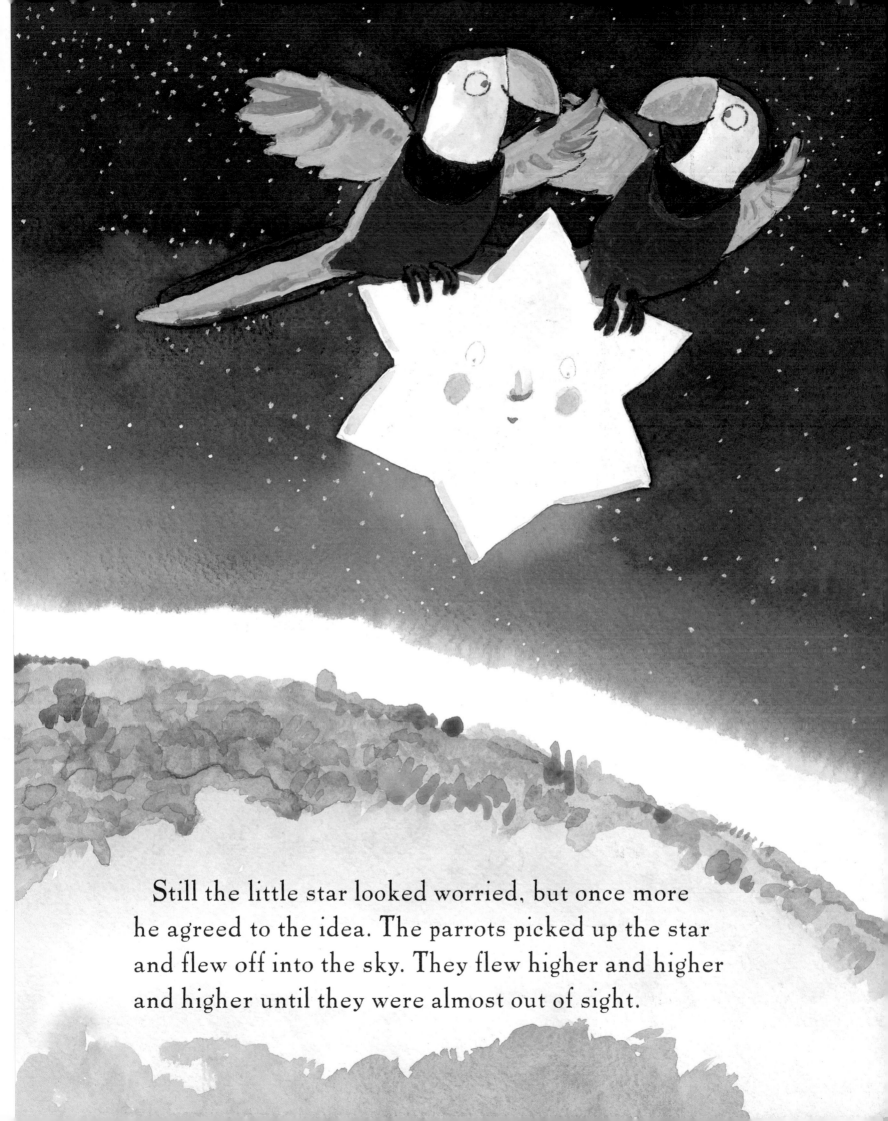

Still the little star looked worried, but once more
he agreed to the idea. The parrots picked up the star
and flew off into the sky. They flew higher and higher
and higher until they were almost out of sight.

Eventually, in a very quiet voice, Harold said, "*I do.*"
The animals all looked at Harold. "We'll build a rocket
to take the little star back to his friends. Everyone
knows that rockets are the best way to get to the stars!"

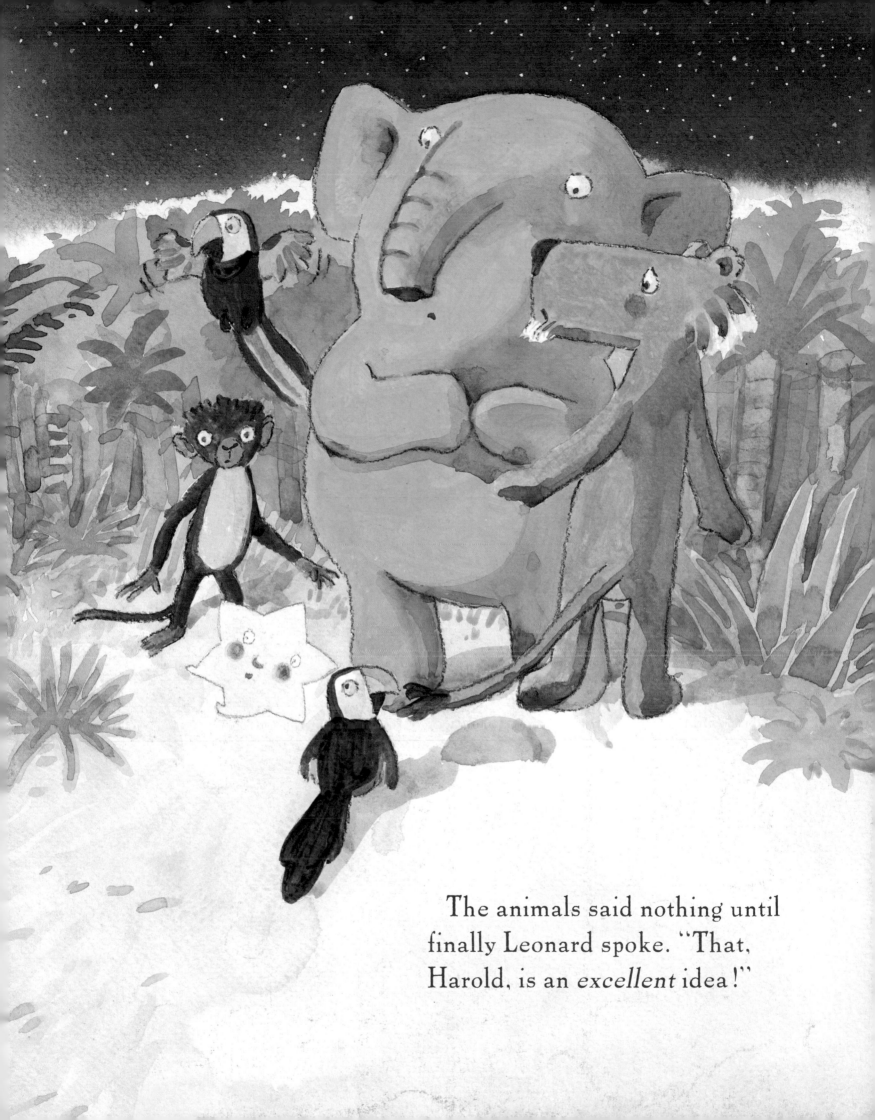

The animals said nothing until
finally Leonard spoke. "That,
Harold, is an *excellent* idea!"

For the next two days
the animals worked on the
rocket until it was ready.

They became great friends with the little star who told them all about the other stars and how beautiful the earth looked from space. When it was time for Harold to take the little star back, the animals were very sad.

Just before the little star
and Harold climbed into
the rocket, Percy and
Pandora gave them special
helmets they'd made from
coconut shells.

And Milly Monkey
gave them a bunch
of bananas to eat
on their trip.

Then, Harold, who was
very proud of his idea,
climbed into the rocket to
take the little star home.

The rocket took off and rose slowly into the sky.

After a while it began to speed up and soon it was racing into space! The other animals watched until the rocket had disappeared from view.

That night, Harold
returned. The animals were
really pleased to see him.
"Well done, Harold!"
they chanted.
"I couldn't have done it
without all of you!" replied
Harold, very shyly.
And as they all gazed
up into the darkness . . .

there in the sky they saw
the little star, twinkling
happily beside his friends!

Other Gullane Children's Books
for you to enjoy . . .

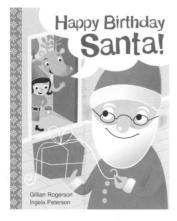

Happy Birthday Santa!

Gillian Rogerson • Ingela Peterson

Pugwug and Little

Susie Jenkin-Pearce •

Tina Macnaughton

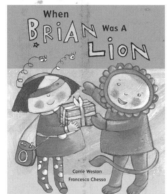

When Brian Was A Lion

Carrie Weston • Francesca Chessa

Not Old Enough

Charlotte Middleton

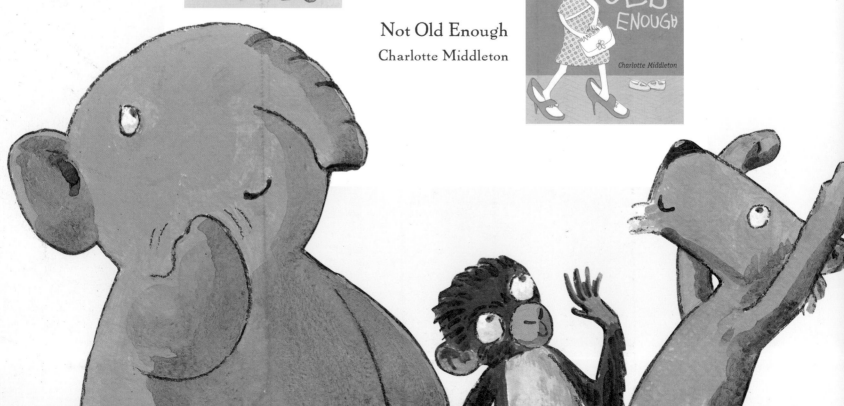